THE BOOKS OF
Ezra
and
Nehemiah

GoodMorningGirls.org

Welcome to Good Morning Girls! We are so glad you are joining us.

God created us to walk with Him, to know Him, and to be loved by Him. He is our living well, and when we drink from the water He continually provides, His living water will change the entire course of our lives.

Jesus said: "Whoever drinks of the water that I will give him will never be thirsty again. The water that I will give him will become in him a spring of water welling up to eternal life." ~ John 4:14 (ESV)

So let's begin.

The method we use here at GMG is called the **SOAK** method.

- **S**—The S stands for *Scripture*—Read the chapter for the day. Then choose 1-2 verses and write them out word for word. (There is no right or wrong choice—just let the Holy Spirit guide you.)

- **O**—The O stands for *Observation*—Look at the verse or verses you wrote out. Write 1 or 2 observations. What stands out to you? What do you learn about the character of God from these verses? Is there a promise, command or teaching?

- **A**—The A stands for *Application*—Personalize the verses. What is God saying to you? How can you apply them to your life? Are there any changes you need to make or an action to take?

- **K**—The K stands for *Kneeling in Prayer*—Pause, kneel and pray. Confess any sin God has revealed to you today. Praise God for His word. Pray the passage over your own life or someone you love. Ask God to help you live out your applications.

SOAK God's word into your heart and squeeze every bit of nourishment you can out of each day's scripture reading. Soon you will find your life transformed by the renewing of your mind!

Walk with the King!

Courtney

WomenLivingWell.org, GoodMorningGirls.org

Join the GMG Community

Share your daily SOAK on **Facebook.com/GoodMorningGirlsWLW**

Instagram.com/WomenLivingWell #WomenLivingWell

GMG Bible Coloring Chart

COLORS	KEYWORDS
PURPLE	God, Jesus, Holy Spirit, Saviour, Messiah
PINK	women of the Bible, family, marriage, parenting, friendship, relationships
RED	love, kindness, mercy, compassion, peace, grace
GREEN	faith, obedience, growth, fruit, salvation, fellowship, repentance
YELLOW	worship, prayer, praise, doctrine, angels, miracles, power of God, blessings
BLUE	wisdom, teaching, instruction, commands
ORANGE	prophecy, history, times, places, kings, genealogies, people, numbers, covenants, vows, visions, oaths, future
GRAY	Satan, sin, death, hell, evil, idols, false teachers, hypocrisy, temptation

Introduction to the Book of Ezra

In the Book of Ezra, we see God's faithfulness even in times when the children of Israel were unfaithful. God had promised that the exiled would return to their land of promise, and he was faithful to keep his promise.

The Book of Ezra details the events surrounding the return of the exiled Jews back to Jerusalem and the rebuilding of the Temple. While Ezra contains only ten chapters, it covers the return of captives to Jerusalem under Zerubbabel and Ezra, as well as over eighty years of events during this very important time in Israel's history. We see that God sent faithful prophets, Haggai and Zechariah, to call them back to their very important task when discouragement led them to halt the reconstruction project.

The name Ezra most likely means, "The Lord Has Helped", and indeed he helped the children of Israel return to their homeland and rebuild the temple despite opposition. Through all this we see God as a God of hope and restoration. Though we may face consequences for our wrong choices in life, God will never forsake us. In his love, he forgives and restores.

The Purpose: Ezra recalls the events of the first post-exilic return of the children of Israel to Jerusalem under Zerubbabel and Ezra, and the rebuilding of the Temple.

The Author: Although the author is anonymous, it is believed that Ezra wrote the book, or at the very least compiled it.

Time Period: This book was written around 538-400 BC.

Key Verse: Ezra 3:11

And they sang responsively, praising and giving thanks to the Lord,
"For he is good, for his steadfast love endures forever toward Israel."
And all the people shouted with a great shout when they praised the Lord,
because the foundation of the house of the Lord was laid.

The Outline:
1. **The return of the Children of Israel under Zerubbabel (1-2)**
   A list of the captives who returned to Jerusalem (2:2-58)

2. **The beginning of the restoration of the Temple (3)**

3. **Opposition to the Temple's restoration and the work halted (4)**

4. **Restoration of the Temple resumes (5)**

5. **The completion and dedication of the Temple (6:13-22)**

6. **Ezra arrives (7)**

7. **Genealogy of the captives who returned with Ezra (8:1-14)**

8. **Ezra addresses sin and brings reform (9-10)**

As we read and study the Book of Ezra, we will see God's love and faithfulness on display over and over again. When the children of Israel are discouraged and apathetic, he sends his prophets to encourage them to keep going. When they are, once again, unfaithful to him, he remains faithful them.

The same is true for us today. Though at times we are unfaithful to God, he remains faithful to us. His grace, and forgiveness are unending toward us. He loves us so much!

So, let's get started studying His word. Be sure to set aside at least 15 minutes a day for your reading. I can't wait to see how God reveals himself personally to each of us, as we study the book of Ezra together.

Keep walking with the King!

Courtney

The Lord stirred up the
spirit of Cyrus king of Persia.

Ezra 1:1

Reflection Question:

The inhabitants of Judah had been carried off to Babylon where they had been exiled for decades. In just the first couple of verses of Ezra, we see three fulfilled prophesies from the books of Daniel, Isaiah, and Jeremiah. Daniel prophesied that the Medes and Persians would defeat Babylon. Isaiah prophesied the birth and rise to power of King Cyrus and Jeremiah prophesied that after 70 years of captivity, a remnant would return to Jerusalem. This is what we're reading today!

Cyrus, king of Persia, made a decree that God's people return to the city of Jerusalem and begin rebuilding the Lord's house. After years of rebellion against God, Judah had finally pushed God's hand so far that he allowed Nebuchadnezzar, king of Babylon, to come and defeat Judah and take her captive. He raided the temple, took some of the treasure, and then the city of Jerusalem was destroyed. Over the next 70 years it sat desolate until God moved the heart of King Cyrus to call for all those who would be willing to go and begin rebuilding the temple. He gave them the treasures King Nebuchadnezzar had taken from the temple.

We are the temple of God. When you accepted Jesus as your personal savior, the Holy Spirit came inside of you. What is the condition of the temple of the Lord in your heart? Has it been neglected? Are the treasures that were once there gone? Has it sat desolate, waiting for a revival and renewal of the Lord to come?

If you have been neglecting that secret place in your heart lately, take some time today to renew your commitment to Christ, grab those verses that were once so dear to you, and begin cleansing and refurnishing your heart with God's Word.

Ezra 1

S—The S stands for **Scripture**

O—The O stands for **Observation**

A—The A stands for **Application**

K—The K stands for **Kneeling in Prayer**

Some of the heads of families came to the house of the Lord...

and made freewill offerings.

Ezra 2:68

Reflection Question:

Only a small number of those in exile chose to return to Jerusalem to begin the rebuilding project. Ezra lists about 50,000 who were the heads of their families besides women and children. This fulfilled the prophecy in Jeremiah that only a remnant would return to begin rebuilding Jerusalem. An offering was taken to begin rebuilding the house of the Lord, and the people gave as generously as they were able according to their means.

Restoration of the house of the Lord required a sacrifice and investment on the part of the people and it's the same for us today. If we want to live a life of dedication to the Lord, we must be ready to sacrifice for the Lord. The people gave as they were able. God will not ask you to give what he hasn't first enabled you to give. Is God laying anything on your heart today that perhaps you need to sacrifice for him? Is it time, finances or giving some extra kindness to someone in your life? Perhaps he is wanting you to give of your talents to serve your church or community. Be bold and step up, take that first step to give back to the Lord in whatever way he is calling you to give.

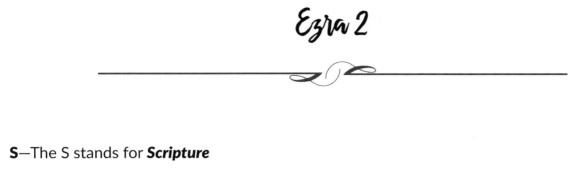

S—The S stands for **Scripture**

O—The O stands for **Observation**

A—The A stands for **Application**

K—The K stands for **Kneeling in Prayer**

For He is good, for his steadfast love

endures forever.

Ezra 3:11

Reflection Question:

For seventy years, Jerusalem had become overgrown and in ruins, but the remnant had returned. Before they even began reconstruction on the temple, Zerubbabel, the political leader of the remnant, and Jeshua, the spiritual leader, built an altar on its ancient foundation and began offering sacrifices and keeping the feasts according to the Law. Soon, materials were ordered, and the builders laid the foundation stones for the temple.

It was a moment to celebrate, with the priests wearing their robes and carrying trumpets, and the Levites with their cymbals. They sang and praised the Lord because worship to God was being restored in Jerusalem again. However, there was a mixed response. The old men, who had seen the first temple, wept loudly; perhaps because they realized that the new temple wouldn't be as luxurious as the one Solomon built.

Is there an area in your life that God is restoring? We can respond to restoration in two ways: we can rejoice and praise him for his wonderful work, or we can weep with regret over what could have been. Looking back with regret prevents us from seeing glory and significance of God's work in our life now. Are you living in regret over something in your past instead of worshiping God for what he is doing in your life today? Read the last four verses of this chapter again, and purpose in your heart to walk forward in praise and worship and leave your regrets over the past behind.

S—The S stands for ***Scripture***

O—The O stands for ***Observation***

A—The A stands for ***Application***

K—The K stands for ***Kneeling in Prayer***

Then the work on the house of God... stopped.

Ezra 4:24

Reflection Question:

Work on the temple had begun, and as often happens, the enemy sent a distraction. When Assyria conquered the northern kingdom, they scattered the Jewish people throughout the world and they themselves settled in the land. After some time, they invited priests to teach them the worship of God but continued to worship their own idols as well. These became known as Samaritans in Jesus' day. These men approached Zerubbabel and Jeshua, offering to help rebuild the temple, but they refused the help, wanting to keep the building of God's house pure and undefiled.

Having been rejected, these men began an active campaign to discourage the workers and stop the work on the temple. This campaign of resistance stretched even into the time of Nehemiah. Eventually, a letter is sent to King Artaxerxes full of false accusations against the remnant rebuilding Jerusalem and the King replied demanding the work be stopped.

Whenever God begins a great work in our life, we can expect the enemy to revolt. He will do everything he can to prevent God's work. But we read in the final verse of this chapter that the work on Jerusalem was only stopped for a time. It will eventually resume. What is the enemy doing to prevent God's work in your life from taking place? Are you discouraged? In Ephesians 6:10-20, we are given armor and weaponry to fight against the enemy and because Christ already won the battle, we fight from a place of victory. Take up your armor and weapons and fight the victorious fight. Don't let the enemy distract you or discourage you any longer!

S—The S stands for **Scripture**

O—The O stands for **Observation**

A—The A stands for **Application**

K—The K stands for **Kneeling in Prayer**

We are the servants of the God of heaven and earth.

Ezra 5:11

Reflection Question:

The rebuilding of the temple has resumed. However, the remnant encounters yet another roadblock. Tattenai, governor of that region, arrives with a group of men demanding to know who they are and who authorized the building of the temple. Tattenai then sends a letter to King Darius requesting that a search be made for the decree issued by King Cyrus authorizing the Jewish people to return to Jerusalem to build the house of God.

When asked by Tattenai who they were, the elders replied, "We are the servants of the God of heaven and earth." Their identity was "servants of God". When God calls us to do something great for him, we can expect to meet opposition. Many times, we become discouraged and even question whether or not what we're doing is really God's will. The enemy will try to cause us to question our identity and our calling, but when we are secure in who we are, we can stand strong on what we know is true and what God has called us to accomplish for him and his kingdom. Are you discouraged right now? Is the enemy causing you to question your calling and the task God has set before you? Take some time today to remind yourself of who you are in Christ. You are a daughter of the King of kings, and he loves you so much!

S—The S stands for **Scripture**

O—The O stands for **Observation**

A—The A stands for **Application**

K—The K stands for **Kneeling in Prayer**

For the Lord had made them joyful.

Ezra 6:22

Reflection Question:

The temple is finally built! The people had faced opposition. They had faced tremendous discouragement that caused them to question the timing of the project and focused instead on building their own houses. God sent them the prophet Haggai to rebuke them and encourage them to press on building God's temple. He and Zechariah encouraged the people to arise from their apathy and depression and complete the work God had called them to do.

The people obeyed the prophets. They repented for building their own comfortable homes while neglecting the house of God. They assigned the priests to their divisions, celebrated the Passover together, and now they are rewarded. The temple of God is completed, and they are joyful.

God's people were made joyful after they obeyed the voice of the prophets and completed the task God had called them to do. The reward for our obedience is joy in God's presence. Think of the last time you obeyed something God was asking of you. Did you feel joy? Is there anything God may be asking of you right now but you feel stuck? Move forward and obey him and experience the joy of the Lord once again!

Ezra 6

S—The S stands for **Scripture**

O—The O stands for **Observation**

A—The A stands for **Application**

K—The K stands for **Kneeling in Prayer**

For Ezra had set his heart to studying

the Law of the Lord and to do it.

Ezra 7:10

Reflection Question:

Finally, Ezra comes on the scene. He is returning to Jerusalem from Babylon with a little under 2,000 men, plus women and children. He received a letter from King Artaxerxes allowing all who wished to return to Jerusalem with Ezra to go, as well as providing him everything else he'd requested. God was giving Ezra favor because he had set his heart on studying God's law. It said he was a skilled scribe and even King Artaxerxes acknowledged that he was filled with God's wisdom.

When we set our hearts to know the word of God, we gain great wisdom. The Proverbs say that the fear of the Lord is the beginning of wisdom. James says that if we lack wisdom, all we need to do is to ask because God gives wisdom generously. It doesn't matter if you are a new Christian, have walked with God most of your life, or you've been away from God for a season and are just coming back to him, God wants us to seek him in his word. Since you are doing this study, I know that you are doing just that. How has your wisdom grown as a result of seeking God and his word? Having knowledge is good but we must remember to live it out in our daily lives. Keep on going! God loves you so much.

S—The S stands for **Scripture**

O—The O stands for **Observation**

A—The A stands for **Application**

K—The K stands for **Kneeling in Prayer**

The hand of our God is for good

on all those who seek him.

Ezra 8:22

Reflection Question:

Ezra and all those who chose to return to Jerusalem are setting out on their journey from Babylon to Jerusalem, a trip that will take approximately four months. As they set out, he encounters a problem. They are carrying with them an enormous amount of wealth and valuables that has been given to them. They needed protection on their journey from potential robbers. Because Ezra had shared with the king about God's power, he felt it would be a bad testimony to then ask for an escort to accompany them for protection. They needed to rely on God to be their protection on this long journey. Ezra divided up the valuables between the Levites and then they set out on their journey. God protected them the entire way and they arrived at Jerusalem safely with all the silver, gold, and valuables that had been given to them.

Ezra had the people humble themselves and fast and pray for protection. Then he proclaimed that the hand of our God is for good on all those who seek him. His words in this chapter echo what Paul said in the book of Romans. Romans 8:28 says that God works all things for good to those who love him and are called according to his purpose. Are you facing a time of uncertainty right now? Perhaps you don't know what to do. Are you in the middle of a difficult situation where you or a loved one needs protection in an area of their life? Seek God. His hand is for good on those who seek him. His promise is that no matter what we're facing, or how dire things look right now, he will turn it for good and for his glory.

S—The S stands for **Scripture**

O—The O stands for **Observation**

A—The A stands for **Application**

K—The K stands for **Kneeling in Prayer**

O Lord, you are just.

Ezra 9:15

Reflection Question:

Ezra's joy at arriving in Jerusalem quicky dissipates as the leaders come and tell him that the people have broken God's command to not intermarry with the pagan nations around them. Even the priests and Levites had begun to intermarry. Ezra is devastated and appalled. God had supernaturally delivered them from their captivity, and they had returned to Jerusalem with the full blessing of the king. Despite their hardship, they had rebuilt the temple, and are now rebuilding the city. Ezra has arrived with a second group of Jews, carrying tremendous wealth and valuables. However, despite God's great victory, they have not remained faithful, but instead are intermarrying with the pagan nations around them.

Not only had the people intermarried with the pagan nations, but they had begun to even embrace some of the idolatry of the nations around them. Less than 100 years have passed, and the people are repeating the same sin that had resulted in them being taken captive. Many times, we are most vulnerable right after a great victory, and the enemy takes this opportunity to lay a trap in our path. Have you been guilty of falling into an old sin from which God had previously delivered you? Do as Ezra did, get down on your knees and repent from that sin, cry out to him for mercy and healing. He promises that when we do, he will hear and restore us.

S—The S stands for **Scripture**

O—The O stands for **Observation**

A—The A stands for **Application**

K—The K stands for **Kneeling in Prayer**

Arise, be strong, and do it.

Ezra 10:4

Reflection Question:

While Ezra is praying and weeping before God for the sin of his nation, a large number of the people gather and begin weeping with him. The last 26 verses list the names of the many priests who had taken pagan wives, some of whom had children by these wives. Then, one of the men, Shechaniah, stands up and calls the people to repentance and restoration. The people realized that if God was to turn toward them again, they must take radical steps of obedience and purge their land and their homes of the pagan influences they had invited.

Repentance of sin always requires radical obedience to God's word. Even a little sin left unchecked will eventually spread and infect every area of our lives. When Shechaniah addressed the people, he encouraged them "Arise, be strong, and do it." Signifying that action and courage would be needed if they were to follow through with what God had already commanded. Is there an area of your life where radical obedience is needed? Be strong and follow through with what you know God is asking of you. If you will arise, be strong, and do it, God will help you.

S—The S stands for *Scripture*

O—The O stands for *Observation*

A—The A stands for *Application*

K—The K stands for *Kneeling in Prayer*

Introduction to the Book of Nehemiah

The Book of Nehemiah details the events surrounding rebuilding the walls of Jerusalem and restoring worship in the temple that was rebuilt under Ezra. Originally, the Book of Nehemiah was included in the Book of Ezra as one book, but when the Bible was translated into Latin, the two books were separated.

Nehemiah's name means, "Yahweh Comforts", and we see how God uses Nehemiah to bring the children of Israel comfort as they read the Law for the first time in the newly restored Temple, and they comprehend how far they had strayed from God's commands.

In the Book of Nehemiah, we follow along as the children of Israel begin the enormous job of rebuilding the walls of Jerusalem in only 52 days. With Nehemiah's expert leadership, they were able to complete this God-given task despite heavy opposition from their enemies, physical weariness, discouragement, and even attempts of direct sabotage through deception and manipulation.

The Purpose: Nehemiah details the determined spirit of God's people as they undertake the daunting task of rebuilding the walls of Jerusalem so that the returning captives can once again live in their land of promise.

The Author: Although the author is anonymous, it is believed that Nehemiah wrote portions of the book and that Ezra helped to compiled and even write it.

Time Period: This book was written around 423 BC.

Key Verse: Nehemiah 8:10

Then he said to them, "Go your way. Eat the fat and drink sweet wine and send portions to anyone who has nothing ready, for this day is holy to our Lord. And do not be grieved, for the joy of the Lord is your strength."

The Outline:
1. Nehemiah's prayer for the people (1)

2. King Artaxerxes sends Nehemiah to Judah (2:1-10)

3. Nehemiah assesses the ruined walls (2:11-20)

4. The children of Israel begin rebuilding the walls (3)

5. Opposition is met (4-6:14)

6. The walls are completed (6:15-7:3)

7. Genealogy of the captives who returned (7:6-73)

8. Ezra reads the Law and the people confess their sins (8-9:3)

9. The Levites seal a new covenant (9:5-10:39)
    A list of those who sealed the covenant (10:1-27)

10. A list of those dwelling in Jerusalem (11)
    A list of those dwelling outside of Jerusalem (11:25-36)

11. A list of the priests and Levites (12:1-26)

12. Dedication of the wall and a cleansing of the temple and people (12:27-13:31)

As we read and study the Book of Nehemiah, we are inspired by the determination and faithful leadership of Nehemiah to lead God's people to take on and successfully complete a seemingly impossible task, even in the face of strong opposition.

This serves as a reminder to us today. As we seek to live dedicated lives that testify of God's love and faithfulness, we can expect to face temptation, discouragement, and temptation. However, it is encouraging to know that we don't live this life alone. We live each day by the power of the Holy Spirit who leads and guides us, and gives us the power we need to daily walk in the purpose for which God created us.

So, let's get started studying His word. Be sure to set aside at least 15 minutes a day for your reading. I can't wait to see how God reveals himself personally to each of us, as we read the book of Nehemiah together.

Keep walking with the King!

Courtney

O Lord, let your ear be attentive

to the prayer of your servants

who delight to fear your name.

Nehemiah 1:11

Reflection Question:

Fifteen years have passed since the end of the book of Ezra and over 70 years since an attempt was made to rebuild the walls of Jerusalem in Ezra 4. Their enemies had successfully prevented them from rebuilding the walls and the remnant has been living in unwalled, unprotected territory, with no defense or protection. God, in his divine wisdom, raised up Nehemiah who lives and serves in the king's palace as his cupbearer, which also allows him to be an unofficial counsel to the king.

While Nehemiah has position and influence in the king's palace, he is deeply concerned about the people in Jerusalem and asks Hanai, one of the brethren, about the situation there. The report is not good. The people are distressed and scorned by their enemies, and the walls and gates are still in ruins. Nehemiah is devastated. His first response is to fast and pray in his sorrow.

His mourning doesn't lead him to defeat, to hopelessness, or to sit and make a plan of action; his mourning leads him to God's throne in prayer and intercession for his people. Have you had bad news recently? Maybe life has taken a difficult turn and you're not sure what to do. Instead of allowing life's troubles lead to you to hopelessness and defeat, let them lead you to God's throne in prayer and petition. Write you prayer below to God

S—The S stands for **_Scripture_**

O—The O stands for **_Observation_**

A—The A stands for **_Application_**

K—The K stands for **_Kneeling in Prayer_**

The God of heaven will make us prosper.

Nehemiah 2:20

Reflection Question:

Nehemiah served as one of the King's high officials – his cupbearer. One day, as the King noticed that Nehemiah was grieved, Nehemiah had the opportunity to share with the King about his city and ask for permission to go and begin rebuilding the walls of Jerusalem. The King granted his request and sent Nehemiah on his journey with written permission for his journey. But Nehemiah is met with opposition.

It is significant to note that Nehemiah met opposition only when he acted on God's call. Opposition didn't come as he prayed and wept, or even as he planned and requested permission from the King. It was while he was in the act of going to Jerusalem that he faced opposition from the enemy.

When we take the step of faith from praying and planning to acting on God's call, we should expect opposition. But this didn't stop Nehemiah from going forward. Rather, he let his enemies know that they had no right in Jerusalem and to step aside because Nehemiah and the people were moving forward. God was going to make them prosper. Is there an area in your life where you are facing opposition right now? Name that area. Are you allowing it to discourage you and cause you to question what you once knew God called you to do for him? Do as Nehemiah did and take a bold stand on what you know is true. Tell the enemy to step aside, because you are going to move forward in God's call and plan for your life. God is with you and he will help you.

S—The S stands for ***Scripture***

O—The O stands for ***Observation***

A—The A stands for ***Application***

K—The K stands for ***Kneeling in Prayer***

Shallum...repaired the next section

with the help of his daughters.

Nehemiah 3:12

Reflection Question:

The work of rebuilding the walls of Jerusalem has begun. Immediately we see Nehemiah's tremendous leadership ability in motivating 40 groups of people to work, each taking a section of the wall. Some were builders, others had different skills, but they all worked together in unity for one purpose and God used anyone willing to work.

As Nehemiah met with the people, he laid out a careful plan for how they would accomplish this enormous task of rebuilding the walls of Jerusalem. There are those who are prone to thinking that making plans isn't very spiritual. Surprisingly, the Bible has a lot to say about God's plans. Planning does not show a lack of faith as long as we lay down our own in surrender to his divine and perfect plans.

Are you a planner? Do you tend to make your plans on your own without thinking of God and what he thinks of your plans? If there is anything you are planning right now in your life, pray over your plans and ask the Lord for direction.

S—The S stands for *Scripture*

O—The O stands for *Observation*

A—The A stands for *Application*

K—The K stands for *Kneeling in Prayer*

Remember the Lord,

who is great and awesome.

Nehemiah 4:14

Reflection Question:

The Jews have made great progress in rebuilding the walls of Jerusalem. They have the whole wall constructed up to half its height. To keep God's people from succeeding in what God had called them to do, Sanballat seeks to discourage them by mocking them and their efforts. He gathers others around him, and they begin to threaten to attack the Jews and create confusion

The enemy's tactics haven't changed with time. Whenever we set our heart and mind to fulfill the plans he's purposed for us, the enemy will try to discourage us. When that doesn't succeed, he plans an attack to confuse and distract us. The question is, how will we respond? Nehemiah responded by encouraging his people to remember God's greatness and be ready to fight. They continued to labor with their weapons ready, always alert for the enemy's attack.

This is a realistic picture of what the Christian walk should look like. We labor for God's kingdom while armed and alert for the enemy's attack. We have no need to fear, He has given us everything we need to live this life with joy and victory. Are you feeling discouraged right now? Has the enemy been trying to distract and confuse you? Take some time today to remind yourself of God's attributes, then take up the armor of God and fight in his strength.

Nehemiah 4

S—The S stands for **Scripture**

O—The O stands for **Observation**

A—The A stands for **Application**

K—The K stands for **Kneeling in Prayer**

Remember for my good, O my God,

all that I have done for this people.

Nehemiah 5:19

Reflection Question:

Where the enemy could not stop God's people from rebuilding the walls by bringing discouragement and confusion from the outside, he succeeded by causing problems from within. Economic downturn, famine and high taxes had left families destitute to the point where they were selling their own children as slaves in order to survive. In this chapter, we read nothing about the wall being built, which suggests that work on the wall had halted due to the discouragement and despair of the people.

When Nehemiah heard the outcry of the people, he was angry. The wealthier among them, including the priests, were taking advantage of their own people by buying up the land of those less fortunate, loaning money at high interest and enslaving their own people. He rebuked the rulers and called on them to restore to these people what had been taken.

Nehemiah showed extraordinary love and honor for God by loving and honoring the people God had called him to lead. Are you allowing distractions of the enemy to prevent you from walking faithfully in the call God has given you? Nehemiah refused to allow the enemy to distract him. He kept his focus on God and the purpose that was laid out for him. If you've been distracted lately, take some time to remember the purpose God has laid out for your life, and rededicate yourself to fulfilling that purpose.

S—The S stands for **Scripture**

O—The O stands for **Observation**

A—The A stands for **Application**

K—The K stands for **Kneeling in Prayer**

But now, O God, strengthen my hands.

Nehemiah 6:9

Reflection Question:

Nehemiah's enemies had done everything they could to stop God's people from rebuilding the walls, and nothing had worked. So, they turned to even greater intimidation and manipulation techniques. They sent a letter to Nehemiah requesting a meeting, to which he replied that he was busy and could not meet with them. After 3 more attempts of the same letter, and receiving the same response, they finally sent a letter accusing him of a planned rebellion in an attempt to intimidate him into stopping the project. But Nehemiah refused to be intimidated. When the letters did not work, they sent an informer as a false prophet to strike fear and entice Nehemiah to seek shelter in the Temple. However, God gave Nehemiah discernment. He recognized this new distraction for what it was and refused to halt the work God had called him to do.

Finally, the walls are completed, and it only took 52 days despite the attacks, discouragement, and distraction of their enemies. They are forced to recognize that God has done this work. Oh friends! We serve an awesome God! What tactics is the enemy using against you right now to make you fearful? Do you need discernment to recognize the plan of the enemy to create fear in your heart? Ask God for wisdom and strength. He will grant it to you so that like Nehemiah, you can stand strong and bold and fulfill the work God has given you to do.

S—The S stands for ***Scripture***

O—The O stands for ***Observation***

A—The A stands for ***Application***

K—The K stands for ***Kneeling in Prayer***

*He was a more faithful
and God-fearing man than many.*

Nehemiah 7:2

Reflection Question:

The walls are rebuilt, the gates are hung, and a great victory has been won, but that doesn't mean God's people get to sit back and rest. Nehemiah turns over the leadership of Jerusalem to Hanani, his brother, and Hananiah. When describing Hananiah, he doesn't list his education, successes, or capabilities. Nehemiah says that Hananiah was faithful and feared the Lord more than many. This was more important than anything else Hananiah could do.

Nehemiah also stationed guards at the gates, at various stations around the wall, and in front of his own house. Just because a victory had been won did not mean they were free from the threat of their enemies. Maintaining victory would mean being led by the fear of the Lord and appointing wise guards at the walls to protect them from intruders.

It is the same in our Christian walk. Winning victories does not mean an end to the enemy's threats. We have to guard our heart from an unexpected attack from the enemy. In what ways do you need to guard your heart today from the enemy? How can you protect yourself from giving into temptation?

S—The S stands for *Scripture*

O—The O stands for *Observation*

A—The A stands for *Application*

K—The K stands for *Kneeling in Prayer*

Do not be grieved

for the joy of the Lord is your strength.

Nehemiah 8:10

Reflection Question:

The children of Israel are gathered together in an open square for a unified purpose, to hear Ezra read to them the Law of the Lord. Special men were appointed to help the people understand what was being read, as having been in exile for 70 years, most of the people had never heard the Law. As he is reading, the people begin to weep with conviction and Nehemiah encourages them to allow the joy of the Lord to fill their hearts.

They had realized the error of their ways, they had wept and mourned in repentance, and now it was time to rejoice. It was a day of restoration and renewal for the children of Israel. When you read God's word, do you feel conviction in your heart? That is one reason God gave us his word: for reproof. But once we have felt the conviction of the Holy Spirit and repented of our sin, then comes times of rejoicing. God does not convict us and expect us to remain sorrowful for our sin. He convicts us to restore us – to restore his joy in our hearts. That is why Paul said in Romans 8:1, that there is therefore now no condemnation for those who are in Christ Jesus, who walk not after the flesh but after the Spirit. When God removes our sin, he removes the sorrow for our sin and replaces it with his joy that gives us strength.

Have you been living under a burden of condemnation over past sins for which God has already forgiven you? Do not be grieved any longer, for the joy of the Lord is your strength. Let him fill you with his joy today!

Nehemiah 8

S—The S stands for **Scripture**

O—The O stands for **Observation**

A—The A stands for **Application**

K—The K stands for **Kneeling in Prayer**

But you are a God ready to forgive, gracious and merciful, slow to anger and abounding in steadfast love.

Nehemiah 9:17

Reflection Question:

The wall has been built, the gates are hung, the Law has been read, and the people have committed to walking in obedience to it. They have set aside a season for fasting and prayer, in repentance of their sin and the sins of their fathers. For one-fourth of the day, they once again listened to the Book of the Law, and one-fourth of the day they confessed and worshipped God. Then, some of the Levites stood up and began to pray, rehearsing God's faithfulness to His people who had repeatedly been unfaithful to him.

Despite Israel's unfaithfulness to God, God had been faithful to them. It is because of God's faithfulness that they were even standing there that day, renewing their covenant with God with their pledge sealed by the priests, Levites, and leaders.

It is the kindness of God that leads us to repentance; his faithfulness that continues to draw us back to him, even when we're unfaithful to him. Have you wavered in your faithfulness to God lately? How are you encouraged to remember that God is faithful, ready to forgive, gracious and merciful, slow to anger and abounding in love for you?

S—The S stands for *Scripture*

O—The O stands for *Observation*

A—The A stands for *Application*

K—The K stands for *Kneeling in Prayer*

We will not neglect the house of our God.

Nehemiah 10:39

Reflection Question:

The children of Israel have renewed their covenant with God, and now the leaders of the land, together with the priests and Levites, seal this covenant. This covenant wasn't at all vague. They specifically stated all of the ways they would obey God's commands and care for the temple. They would be faithful in their relationships with the opposite sex, they would be faithful to honor the Sabbath, and they would be faithful in supporting and caring for God's house.

When we renew our covenant with God, we will soon discover that God requires specific commitments from us in obedience to his Word. His commands range from our commitment to biblical morality and how just we are in our business practices to how well we respect his house. What specific commitments have you made to God lately? Is there an area of your life where God is seeking a greater level of commitment from you?

S—The S stands for *Scripture*

O—The O stands for *Observation*

A—The A stands for *Application*

K—The K stands for *Kneeling in Prayer*

And the people blessed all the men

who willingly offered to live in Jerusalem.

Nehemiah 11:2

Reflection Question:

Jerusalem has gone from being a city in ruins to having the temple rebuilt under the direction of Ezra. The walls were repaired under the leadership of Nehemiah and a remnant returned and renewed her covenant with the Lord. But more was needed. The threat of enemy attack remained, and so there was a great need for more people to live inside of Jerusalem, The city needed a greater population for protection and to continue its restoration.

The leaders already inhabited Jerusalem, and now the people are casting lots for 10% of the outlying population to relocate there as well. On top of this 10%, there were also those who willingly offered to move. This decision came at a cost. Not only were they leaving behind the homes they'd built and established, as well as loved ones and friends, but they were choosing to move to a city that was under greater threat of enemy invasion.

This was a sacrifice they chose to make in order to answer God's call. God's call often comes at great sacrifice. There will be those who will not agree with our decision or who don't understand the sacrifices we make. Choosing to follow God's call makes us a greater target for the enemy's attack. However, as we see in our passage today, there was a special blessing for those who willingly chose to follow God's call; and it's no difference for us today. When we choose to step out in faith and boldness to answer God's call on our life, we will experience a new level of blessing in our life. In what way is God calling you to step out in faith and obedience? Have you answered that call?

S—The S stands for *Scripture*

O—The O stands for *Observation*

A—The A stands for *Application*

K—The K stands for *Kneeling in Prayer*

God had made them rejoice with great joy.

Nehemiah 12:43

Reflection Question:

The day has come to dedicate the wall of Jerusalem. All of the leaders came together with the singers and the people, and they rejoiced, sang, and worshipped God so that the sound of their worship and rejoicing was heard from far away. Before they began to worship, the priests and Levites did a very important thing. They first purified themselves, then purified the people, and purified the gates and walls of the city. This was a very important step before they began worship as they recognized the importance of purity in true worship.

In the Old Testament, they followed rituals of cleansing before meeting with God; but now we are under a new covenant. God is not as concerned with our outward purity as much as he is concerned with purity of heart. We can't purify our own hearts, that's why we need Jesus. In verse 45 we read that purification was an ongoing ritual; and it is no different for us today. We need to daily cleanse our hearts with the cleansing water of the word of God to maintain a pure heart before God, because true worship flows from a pure heart.

When God's people, who are purified and set apart for sacred use, come together in unity to worship God, the power of their collective worship is amplified before God. Has the defilement of this world begun to stick to your heart in some areas? Have you recognized areas of your life where you've made small compromises? Set aside some time today to allow God to purify your heart, and worship him.

S—The S stands for *Scripture*

O—The O stands for *Observation*

A—The A stands for *Application*

K—The K stands for *Kneeling in Prayer*

Remember me, O my God, for good.

Nehemiah 13:31

Reflection Question:

After the Jewish people had experienced this tremendous revival, Nehemiah returned to Babylon for the next 10-12 years. While he was away, Eliashib the priest emptied out a storeroom in the temple courts and gave it to Tobiah to live in. Not only had Tobiah heavily resisted and plotted to thwart the work of God in rebuilding the walls of Jerusalem, he was also an Ammonite and thus forbidden to enter into the assembly.

About a decade later, Nehemiah returns to Jerusalem and what he discovers grieves and angers him. It did not take long for God's people to go back on their promises. They had failed to keep the sabbath. They had failed to bring their tithes, so that the Levites returned to their fields out of necessity. They were intermarrying with the pagan surrounding nations. These were all things that had angered God before and led to their captivity.

How often are we like the children of Israel? We make promises to God in times of personal revival and yet fail to keep those promises and go back to living the way we did before. Is there a promise you've made to God that you have not yet kept? Remember, God is full of mercy and grace; his love is everlasting. When we fail, all we need to do is seek his forgiveness. And he gives it freely! Purpose today to remain faithful to God.

S—The S stands for *Scripture*

O—The O stands for *Observation*

A—The A stands for *Application*

K—The K stands for *Kneeling in Prayer*

Made in the USA
Middletown, DE
10 January 2024